Dear Parent:

Congratulations! Your child is taking the first steps on an exciting journey. The destination? Independent reading!

STEP INTO READING® will help your child get there. The program offers five steps to reading success. Each step includes fun stories and colorful art. There are also Step into Reading Sticker Books, Step into Reading Math Readers, Step into Reading Phonics Readers, Step into Reading Write-In Readers, and Step into Reading Phonics Boxed Sets—a complete literacy program with something to interest every child.

Learning to Read, Step by Step!

Ready to Read   Preschool–Kindergarten
• big type and easy words • rhyme and rhythm • picture clues
For children who know the alphabet and are eager to begin reading.

Reading with Help   Preschool–Grade 1
• basic vocabulary • short sentences • simple stories
For children who recognize familiar words and sound out new words with help.

Reading on Your Own   Grades 1–3
• engaging characters • easy-to-follow plots • popular topics
For children who are ready to read on their own.

Reading Paragraphs   Grades 2–3
• challenging vocabulary • short paragraphs • exciting stories
For newly independent readers who read simple sentences with confidence.

Ready for Chapters   Grades 2–4
• chapters • longer paragraphs • full-color art
For children who want to take the plunge into chapter books but still like colorful pictures.

STEP INTO READING® is designed to give every child a successful reading experience. The grade levels are only guides. Children can progress through the steps at their own speed, developing confidence in their reading, no matter what their grade.

Remember, a lifetime love of reading starts with a single step!

*For my boy, Luther, and his buddy
Asher—it's fun watching you two
together. —C.M.H.*

*For my son, Ryan, who is learning to
eat his veggies. —B.S.*

Text copyright © 2012 by Charise Mericle Harper
Cover and interior illustrations copyright © 2012 by Bob Shea

Visit us on the Web!
StepIntoReading.com
randomhouse.com/kids
Educators and librarians, for a variety of teaching tools, visit us at
randomhouse.com/teachers

Library of Congress Cataloging-in-Publication Data
Harper, Charise Mericle.
Wedgieman: a hero is born / by Charise Mericle Harper ; illustrated by Bob Shea.
p. cm. — (The adventures of Wedgieman)
  Summary: Veggieboy practices flying, lifting, and helping people to hone his superhero skills, and finally Veggieman's training as a superhero is complete, but he is surprised when children want to change his name.
  ISBN 978-0-307-93071-2 (trade paperback) — ISBN 978-0-375-97058-0 (Gibraltar library binding)
[1. Superheroes—Fiction. 2. Vegetables—Fiction. 3. Growth—Fiction.] I. Shea, Bob, ill. II. Title.
PZ7.H231323We 2012 [E]—dc23 2011016352

Printed in the United States of America   10 9 8 7 6 5 4 3 2 1

STEP INTO READING®
STEP 3

WEDGIEMAN: a HERO is BORN

The ADVENTURES of
WEDGIEMAN

By Charise Mericle Harper

Illustrated by Bob Shea

Random House New York

One day a superhero was born.

His name was Veggiebaby,

and he was very hungry.

He ate vegetables, lots of them,

even the green ones.

The tiny round

ones were his

favorite.

There was a big sign on Veggiebaby's wall. Veggiebaby looked at it.

"GAAAA!" said Veggiebaby.

He played with his food anyway.

He was good at it.

He made broccoli bears,

 tomato tigers,

spinach spiders,

and even giant
green-bean
gorillas.

Veggiebaby was brave.

He wasn't scared of vegetables, no matter what they looked like.

He just drooled, looked them in the eye,

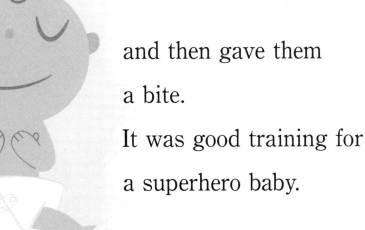

and then gave them a bite.
It was good training for a superhero baby.

Babies are messy eaters.

Superhero babies are super-messy eaters.

When Veggiebaby ate lunch, there was

food everywhere.

There were carrots covering the carpet.

There was squash on the sofa.

There were peas in his pants.

And sometimes, there was even

cabbage on the cat.

The cat did not like cabbage.

All the vegetables made Veggiebaby
very healthy.

He grew fast, and one day he turned
into Veggieboy.

Veggieboy said, "I must practice
my superhero skills."
He practiced flying.
It was not easy.

One day he spent nearly three hours
stuck on the ceiling.

It was a lot easier to go up than
to come down.

He practiced lifting.

He held a tree full of chattering
squirrels high in the air.

He held a bus full of chattering
grandmas high in the air.
"I can do more," said Veggieboy.
"Who wants to go next?"
Suddenly, there was silence.
Not everyone likes to look down
from the sky.

He practiced looking with his
X-ray eyes.

Not everyone was happy about that.

Not even Veggieboy.

Some things are better not seen.

He practiced
shape-shifting.

"I am a hamster!"
said Veggieboy.
Nothing
happened.

"I am a robot!"
said Veggieboy.

Nothing happened.

"I guess I can't
shape-shift,"
said Veggieboy.
He was only a little
bit unhappy.

Mostly, he was hungry.

He thought about carrots.

Suddenly, BAM!

He was a giant carrot.

"Ah!" screamed Veggieboy.

"I look so tasty!"

He quickly changed back.

"That's dangerous!" said Veggieboy.

"I'm only going to use that
in emergencies."

Veggieboy was proud of his super-skills.

And because he was a super*hero,*

he only used them to do good.

On shopping days, he carried groceries and old ladies.

He could find lost keys or missing socks.

And he was always helpful at fairs
and picnics.

LEMONADE
DRINKING
CONTEST

Veggieboy was a very busy helper.

But there was one thing he never forgot.
He always ate his vegetables.

One day Veggieboy turned into
Veggieman.

Veggieman was now a grown-up.

"I need a new superhero outfit,"

he said.

He went to the store.

He tried on lots of outfits.

27

Finally, he said, "I think this is
the one. Now I can help the children
of the world eat their veggies and
be healthy!" He smiled and made
a superhero pose in the mirror.

Suddenly, he heard a scream.

It was a cry for help.

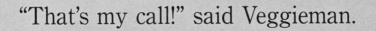

"That's my call!" said Veggieman.

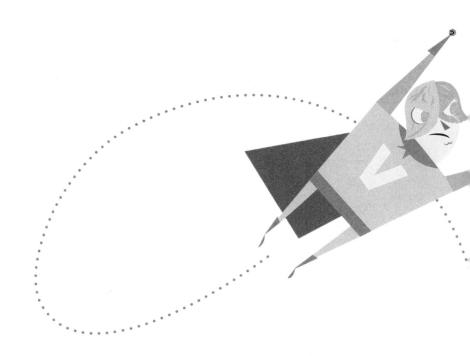

He ran out of the store and flew
into the sky.

Veggieman used his super-ears
to find the sound.
A small boy was stuck high in the
branches of a tree.

HELP ME!

"Help me! Help me!"
cried the boy.

"Save him! Save him!"
cried the children
under the tree.

SAVE
HIM!

SAVE HIM!

"Hang on!" shouted Veggieman.

He grabbed the boy and
carried him safely
to the ground.

"Eat your veggies and you can be strong like me," said Veggieman.

He gave the small boy some carrots.

All the children were happy.

"Yay! Wedgieman! Our hero!"

they cheered.

"No, wait," said Veggieman.

"It's *Veggie*man, not *Wedgie*man!"

"No it isn't!" said the small boy, and

he pointed to Veggieman's chest.

A stick from the tree
was stuck to Veggieman's shirt.
It made his *V* look like a *W*.
Veggieman pulled off the stick.

"Silly children," he said. "It's a *V*, not a *W*. I'm Veggieman."

"I like Wedgieman better," said the boy.

"Yay! Wedgieman!" cheered the children.

Veggieman was confused.

He was not used to children.

Especially children who were wrong

but said they were right.

He thought for a moment

and then smiled.

He pointed to his chest.

"Look, children, even if I made this *V*
into a *W*, it still wouldn't spell *wedgie*.
And that's because *wedgie* has a *D*
in it."

"That's okay," said the children.

"We don't care about spelling.

You can fix it."

And then they ran off to play.

THE END—OR IS IT?

Veggieman walked back to the store.
He was tired and
didn't feel like flying.

He was sorry that he didn't have any
extra carrots or spinach in his pockets.
"This outfit is too loose," he said.
"I need a smaller size."

He pulled up his pants.

A small boy was watching.

The small boy told everyone what he had seen.